Dear Parents and Educators,

Welcome to Penguin Young Readers! As parents and educators, you know that each child develops at his or her own pace—in terms of speech, critical thinking, and, of course, reading. Penguin Young Readers recognizes this fact. As a result, each Penguin Young Readers book is assigned a traditional easy-to-read level (1–4) as well as a Guided Reading Level (A–P). Both of these systems will help you choose the right book for your child. Please refer to the back of each book for specific leveling information. Penguin Young Readers features esteemed authors and illustrators, stories about favorite characters, fascinating nonfiction, and more!

Monkey See, Monkey Do

LEVEL 1

GUIDED READING LEVEL **D**

This book is perfect for an **Emergent Reader** who:
- can read in a left-to-right and top-to-bottom progression;
- can recognize some beginning and ending letter sounds;
- can use picture clues to help tell the story; and
- can understand the basic plot and sequence of simple stories.

Here are some **activities** you can do during and after reading this book:
- Picture Clues: Use the pictures to tell the story. "Read" the illustrations.
- Rhyming Words: On a separate sheet of paper, make a list of all the rhyming words in this story. For example, *eat* rhymes with *feet* so write those two words next to each other.
- Sight Words: Sight words are frequently used words that readers must know just by looking at them. These words are known instantly, on sight. Knowing these words helps children develop into efficient readers. The sight words listed below appear in this book. As you read the story, have the child point out the sight words.

for	go	here	no	the
get	good	my	stop	you

Remember, sharing the love of reading with a child is the best gift you can give!

—Bonnie Bader, EdM, and Katie Carella, EdM
   Penguin Young Readers program

*Penguin Young Readers are leveled by independent reviewers applying the standards developed by Irene Fountas and Gay Su Pinnell in *Matching Books to Readers: Using Leveled Books in Guided Reading*, Heinemann, 1999.

To my two favorite monkeys,
Joe and Tommy—DR

Penguin Young Readers
Published by the Penguin Group
Penguin Group (USA) Inc., 375 Hudson Street, New York, New York 10014, USA
Penguin Group (Canada), 90 Eglinton Avenue East, Suite 700, Toronto, Ontario M4P 2Y3, Canada
(a division of Pearson Penguin Canada Inc.)
Penguin Books Ltd., 80 Strand, London WC2R 0RL, England
Penguin Group Ireland, 25 St. Stephen's Green, Dublin 2, Ireland
(a division of Penguin Books Ltd.)
Penguin Group (Australia), 250 Camberwell Road, Camberwell, Victoria 3124, Australia
(a division of Pearson Australia Group Pty. Ltd.)
Penguin Books India Pvt. Ltd., 11 Community Centre, Panchsheel Park, New Delhi—110 017, India
Penguin Group (NZ), 67 Apollo Drive, Rosedale, Auckland 0632, New Zealand
(a division of Pearson New Zealand Ltd.)
Penguin Books (South Africa) (Pty.) Ltd., 24 Sturdee Avenue, Rosebank,
Johannesburg 2196, South Africa

Penguin Books Ltd., Registered Offices: 80 Strand, London WC2R 0RL, England

Text and illustrations copyright © 2000 by Dana Regan. All rights reserved. First published in 2000
by Grosset & Dunlap, an imprint of Penguin Group (USA) Inc. Published in 2011 by Penguin Young
Readers, an imprint of Penguin Group (USA) Inc., 345 Hudson Street, New York, New York 10014.
Manufactured in China.

Library of Congress Control Number: 00-055143

ISBN 978-0-448-42299-2   10 9 8 7 6 5 4 3

PENGUIN YOUNG READERS

LEVEL 1

EMERGENT READER

Monkey See, Monkey Do

by Dana Regan

Penguin Young Readers
An Imprint of Penguin Group (USA) Inc.

Monkey see,

monkey do.

Can you do

what they do, too?

Monkeys ride

and monkeys skate.

This one does

a figure eight.

Monkeys creep

and monkeys crawl.

I hope that this one

does not fall!

9

Monkeys jump
and monkeys shout.
Monkeys shake
their arms about.

11

Monkeys laugh.

And monkeys cry.

Monkeys smile
and wave bye-bye.

Monkeys run

and monkeys hide.

Look for monkeys

far and wide.

Monkeys kiss

and monkeys hug.

Monkeys do
the jitterbug.

Hop on one foot, hop on two.

You can do what monkeys do!

Can you guess

what monkeys eat?

They eat bananas
with their feet.

Monkeys yawn.

Do not make a peep.

Shhh!

I think

the monkeys are asleep.

Good night.